This book belongs to

____

Dedicated to Aaron, thank you for supporting my dream and helping it become a reality xx

First Published in the United Kingdom in 2018 by Wish Publishing Ltd

www.wishpublishing.co.uk

ISBN 978-1-9996656-2-3

Printed in the UK

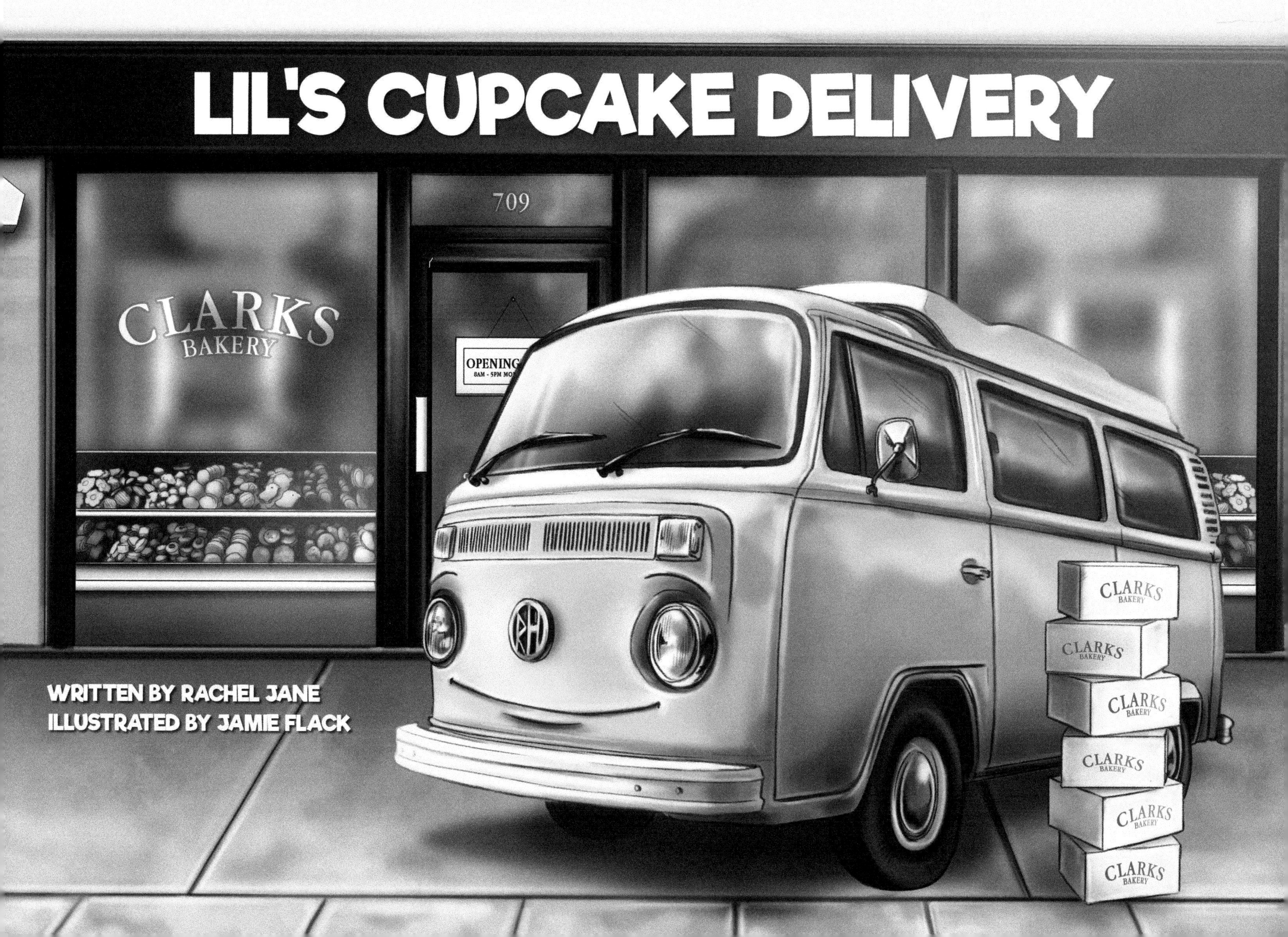
LIL'S CUPCAKE DELIVERY
709
CLARKS
BAKERY
OPENING
WRITTEN BY RACHEL JANE
ILLUSTRATED BY JAMIE FLACK
CLARKS
BAKERY
CLARKS
BAKERY
CLARKS
BAKERY
CLARKS
BAKERY
CLARKS
BAKERY
CLARKS
BAKERY

On a sunny day in the spring,
Lil's excited for what today will bring.

She loves to drive
around the town,
Driving up hills
And racing back down.

Lil loves talking to the people
And seeing what they do,
visiting the shops and cafés
she loves those too.

She listens to the birds
tweet in the park
and will often stay
until it gets dark.

She talks to Mrs. Brown
who handles the post.

And to Mrs. Taylor
Who cooks a great roast.

Then to Mr. Smith
Who sells bolts and screws.

And talks to Mrs. Baker
about all the news.

But Lil's favourite person to go and see
Is Mrs. Clark who runs the bakery.

She loves the smell of her freshly baked cakes,
brownies, cookies and her other great bakes!

She bakes her cakes for all kinds of events,
birthdays, weddings and even presents.

She makes her cakes with love and care,
they are almost too good to share!

There are big cakes and small ones
with icing galore,

Chocolate, vanilla
and so many more!

She decorates her cakes
with sugary flowers,

And stacks them
into beautiful towers.

"Lil, I need to deliver these cakes today,
for 10 events and a birthday.

I can't bake the cakes and deliver them too.
I just don't know what I'm going to do!"

"Mrs. Clark don't worry,
I have a plan
I can be your cupcake
delivery van."

Mrs. Clark packs up and starts to load
boxes of cupcakes, then Lil hits the road.

She drives past the church and out of the town
for her first delivery to Mrs. Brown.

Birthday cupcakes for her young son,
to celebrate him turning one.
"These are perfect for my little man!"
"Just doing my job
as the cupcake van!"
CLARKS
BAKERY
RH

Lil is on her way, back on track,
for her next delivery to Mr. Mack.

There are chocolate cupcakes, red velvet too
for his friends at his leaving do.

"Oh these are delicious,
they're the best cakes.
Better than anyone else makes!"

"You're so right Mr. Mack,
you're such a wise man!
Now I've got to go,
I'm the cupcake van!"

And off Lil goes with a rev and a smile,
she can't believe she's driven for miles!

Lil only has one more to go,
a tall cake tower for the wedding show.

She's cruising and moving and humming along.

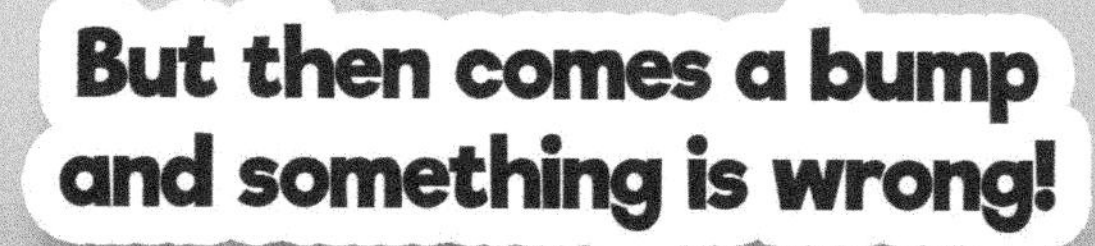

BUMP!

She hears a loud crash and then comes a clatter...

Oh NO! The cake's fallen off the platter!

SPLAT!

Lil starts to panic,
what can she do?
The wedding show needs
the cake at two!

This is not in her plan
as the Cupcake delivery van!

She zooms down the hill
back to the town
Passing Mr. Mack
and then Mrs. Brown.

She keeps zooming
until she can see
Mrs. Clark baking
in her bakery.

"Lil are you ok?
Whatever is the matter?"
"I hit a bump and the cake
fell off the platter!"

"Oh Lil, what a shame, but never fear,
I've just thought of a great idea!

I'm going to make a beautiful tower,
Of all my cupcakes and perfect flowers."

She picks the chocolate and red velvet too.
Banana and lemon to name a few.
Then the flowers, pink and white,
it is such a beautiful sight.

"Lil lets go, I've done all I can,
I need my cupcake delivery van!"

They get to the show with time to spare,
and set up their cupcakes for the fayre.

HOTEL
WEDDING
FAYRE TODAY!
OPEN FROM 2PM!

Everyone arrives for a cake tasting,

"Yum!"
"Delicious!"
"These are amazing!"

“Lil I can’t believe it, what a success!
They think the cupcakes are the best!
I’d love your help every day if you can,
to be my official cupcake van?”

Lil can't help it, she has a huge smile,
she can't wait to deliver in style.

She will do the best that she can
as the official cupcake van.

RH